P9-CMB-934

The Winter Lodge

The Winter Lodge

A White Mountain Mouse Tale

by Gwen Reiss

Illustrated by David North

Printed in the U.S.A.

Designed by Acorn Studio, Glastonbury, Connecticut

ISBN-13 978-0-9815882-0-9
ISBN-10 0-9815882-0-4

For information regarding permissions, please write to:
Salem Street Books, P. O. Box 567, New Canaan, Connecticut 06840

www.salemstreetbooks.com

In memoriam

Rita Campbell North

---

and for Caroline, Daniel, Eliza and Maggie

Chatham Woods Camp is old. Dilapidated cabins lean toward the lake, and the lodge building with its massive cast-iron stove and its flag over the dining-room table opens for a few weeks a year for pancakes and lobster suppers. During those summer weeks, the bang of the screen door echoes over the lake, and canoes slip along the waterside.

In the fall, all is quiet. The mice move in and get into everything. For a while the camp belongs to them …

The autumn sun glowed yellow all around

when Uncle Gar showed us what he'd found.

"For the winter," Uncle Gar said, "I've seen worse."

He jumped, grabbed a wire, and went in first.

We followed him, but were in no rush.

We took the route through pine needles and brush.

My mother was the cautious kind of mouse;

we hid under the corner of the house.

The moon's light turned the ground a silver-white.

Where was he now? We waited through the night.

Shadows crawled and darted all around.

Alert, awake, we listened for each sound.

He reappeared — half pirate, half clown.

For a moment, I was hanging upside-down.

Who knew a sword could fit a mouse's fist?

Mother said he's always been like this.

We entered through a chimney made of stone

and found ourselves (thank goodness!) all alone.

Inside the camp, while mother was resting,

Uncle found some mattress fluff for nesting.

We dove for treasure through a blanket tear.

I got a peanut and a gummy bear.

"Adventure," he said, "is magic and chance."

I love to hear my uncle when he rants.

I wandered to the next room on my own

A huge machine sat quiet as a stone.

I pretended he was the vacuum cleaner king.

Ping pong balls came down on me and him.

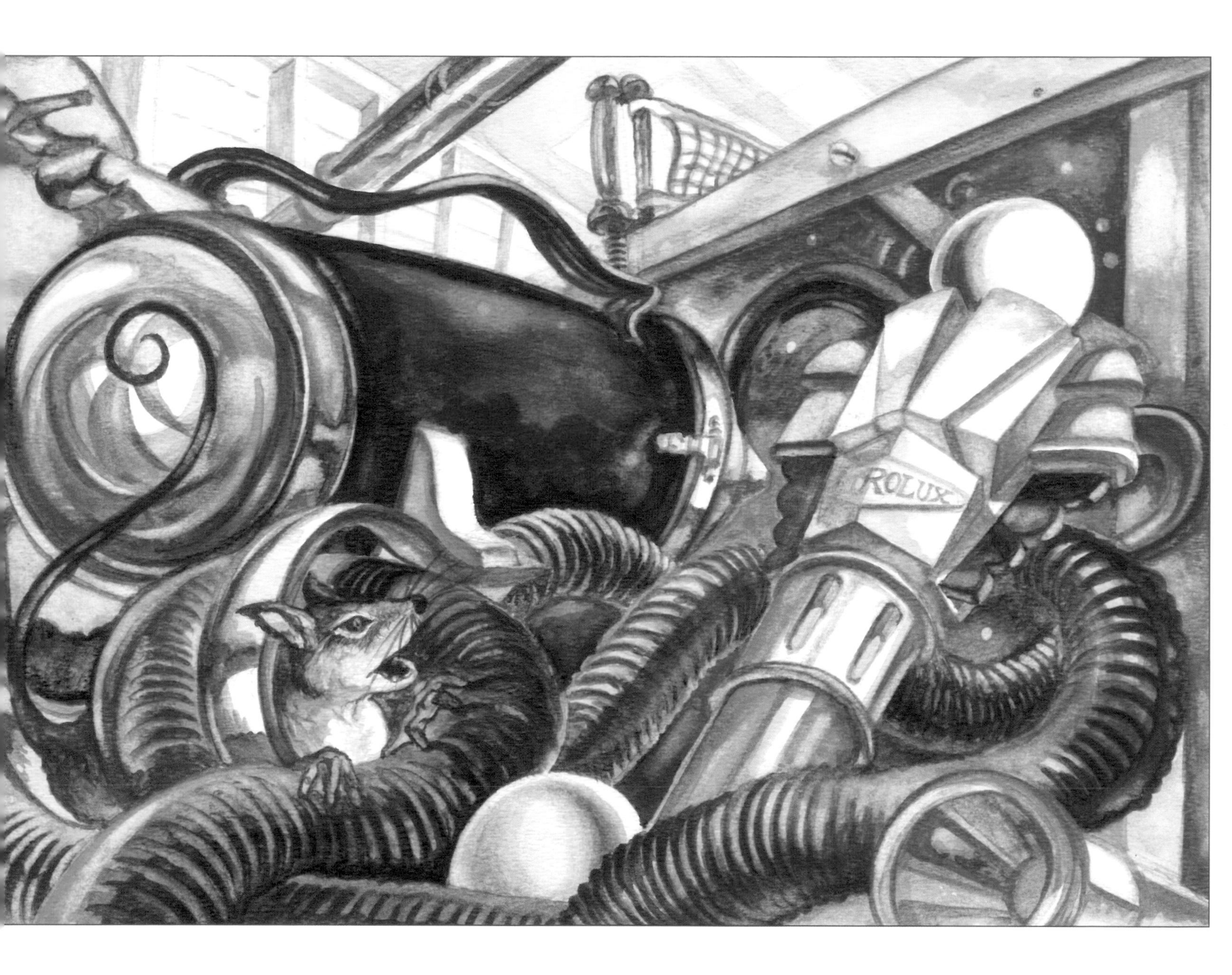
ROLUX

In the kitchen there was shelving to explore.

We tried to move the best stuff to the floor.

"I used to wrestle lobsters," Uncle said.

He took the claw; I took the creature's head.

We searched the other rooms. We heard a snap.

I saw a fish, a raincoat, and a map.

Outside, a fish is never on a board,

and daylight isn't summoned with a cord.

We found a metal racing car in red,

books, mirrors, pictures, games and beds.

I climbed up high where light came through in beams.

I stood and saw myself as in a dream.

It snowed, the night shone bright, the morning glittered.

I built a piece of cheese and a handsome critter.

The trees and ground were white, the sky was blue,

and every path and rooftop looked brand new.

Dinner time was never very formal.

For mice, who could say if this was normal?

Good fortune is a plate that's full — and friends.

But we heard scratching, and we heard the branches bend.

Others came; we thought they'd never leave.

It was a wild and noisy New Year's Eve.

We read the news, then made ourselves some hats.

Don't ask me what happened after that.

FRESH PINE

Our guests departed as quickly as they came —

apologetic, sleep-deprived, and tame.

Old Orkney traveled far; we heard he made it.

And many starry nights we sat and waited ...

Dubhe
PAINT
NOT EAT
TO OPEN
BRAND
WARNING

for the air to warm, for frogs and bugs to wake,

for the return to our old den by the lake.

We traveled in the woods, but never far.

We hoped to spend the summer in the car.

I woke one morning to a mountain scene

and thought the world had never looked so green.

After winter's dark and cloistered hours,

I much prefer the company of flowers.

We left the lodge when temperatures were fair.

It was, we know, a little worse for wear.

July is here; the summer folks moved in.

This morning I went back there for a swim.

The Winter Lodge
was designed using
InDesign on a Mac OS X
with the ITC font Veljovic
at Acorn Studio in Glastonbury,
Connecticut. The book was printed
by Hitchcock Printing Company
of New Britain, Connecticut.